Gimme-Jimmy

by

Sherrill S. Cannon

Illustrations by

Kalpart

Strategic Book Publishing and Rights Co.

Book Design/Layout, Illustrations and Book Cover design by Kalpart
visit www.kalpart.com

Strategic Book Publishing and Rights Co.
12620 FM 1960, Suite A4-507
Houston, TX 77065
www.sbpra.com

ISBN: 978-1-61897-267-5

Dedication

For my daughters
Kerry Elisabeth
&
Cailin Rosemary
who have helped me with their
expertise, advice, concern and love
throughout all my books...
and their lives!

And, as always, for the Grands:
Josh, Parker, Colby,
Lindsay, Tucker,
Kelsey, Mikaila, Kylie,
Cristiano and ?

James Alexander's nickname was Jim,

But nobody would be friends with him.

No one wanted to play with Jimmy,

For Jim Alexander always said, "Gimme."

"Gimme my books," he'd say. "Gimme my toys."

He'd grab from the girls and he'd snatch from the boys.

Jill didn't like him and neither did Jack,

For Jimmy would take things and not give them back.

Jim was a bully at home and at school;

Though nobody liked him, he thought he was cool.

One day his daddy said, "Jimmy, my boy,

You must learn to share, or you'll have little joy.

You'd better be careful, you must understand,

Your greed may show up in the size of your hand.

Your hand will get bigger, the more that you take,

And you will be sorry you made this mistake.

Your poor little hand will continue to grow

Until it will rest on the top of your toe!"

But Jimmy just shrugged and then said, to explain,

"All the kids say Gimme-Jimmy's my name."

When Jimmy woke up bright and early next morn,

He reached for his clock to turn off the alarm.

He noticed the off button seemed very small,

But he was too sleepy to think much at all.

He got dressed for school and went downstairs to eat,

(He had trouble tying the shoes on his feet),

When his dad said, "Would you like cereal, Jimmy?"

He snatched the whole box, while mumbling, "Gimme."

All of a sudden, he felt his hand swell;

It was slowly enlarging and seemed red as well.

It didn't hurt much, but it looked very strange,

And Jimmy could see a remarkable change:

His hand was much larger—as big as his head!

"I think I know why I had trouble," he said,

"Resetting my clock, and tying my shoes—

My fingers are way too big for me to use!

Perhaps I should try not to say the word 'Gimme.'"

His hand twitched and grew again, startling Jimmy.

When he tried to put on his spring jacket for school,

He thought it was lucky it was not very cool.

For his hand had grown larger than he could believe—

It was way far too big to fit into his sleeve!

So Jim went to school without his spring coat,

Hoping his classmates would never take note

That his hand now had swollen to three times its size;

Perhaps his new ball glove would be a disguise!

But when Jimmy tried it, his hand wouldn't fit;

And he cried when he knew he could not use his mitt.

The children all laughed at his gigantic hand,

And Jimmy just knew they would not understand

That no matter what happened, he'd never say, Gimme;

No, he'd learned his lesson, had poor little Jimmy!

His hand had grown heavy and hung by his side;

It was four times as long and five times as wide!

And Jim couldn't write; he could not hold a pen.

His fingers would drop things again and again.

When he used the computer, the keyboard keys

Only produced a succession of Z's;

His hand was too big and his fingers too fat,

When he pushed down on one key, the others went flat!

He couldn't play baseball or put on his clothes;

He even had trouble when blowing his nose.

His hand was so big that it covered his face,

And his head disappeared without even a trace!

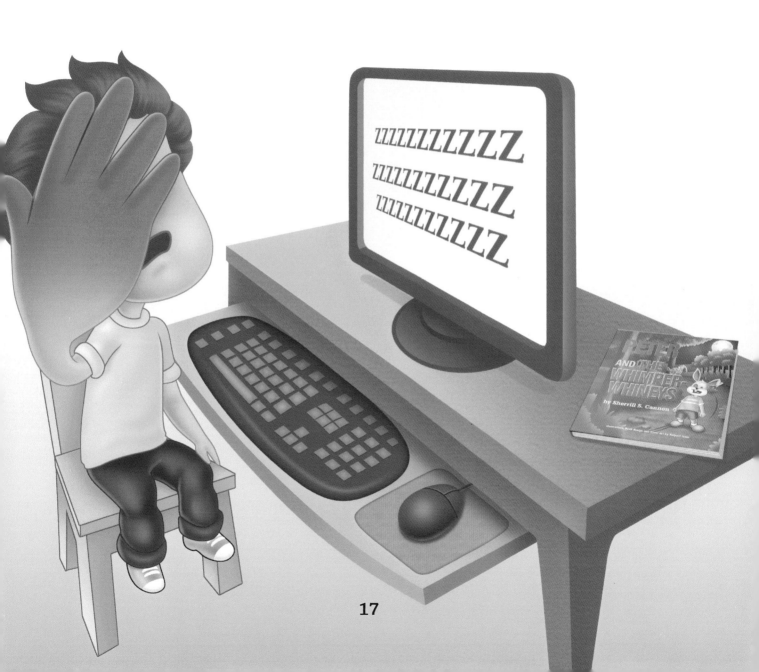

Said Jimmy, "I promise I'll never say, 'Gimme,'"

And then his hand grew almost bigger than Jimmy!

Now his hand rested on top of his shoe,

And Jimmy just didn't know what he should do.

He knew he could not say that horrible word,

For each time he said it, the growing occurred!

His foot was now hurting from all of the weight;

And he couldn't go home now, although it was late.

(If he could drag it across the floor,

He'd never be able to fit through the door!)

He cried, "If I'd only listened to Dad,

I wouldn't be here at the school, feeling sad.

I'd be outside right now with a normal-sized hand . . .

If only I knew how to shrink it again."

Just then in the doorway, his father appeared.

He said to poor Jimmy, "It's as I had feared.

You must have continued to say the word, 'Gimme,'

And now you are more of a hand than a Jimmy!"

"Now you must do what I say, for I think

There might be a way to help your hand shrink.

The only way I know to make your hand right

Is to go out of your way to be very polite.

Always say, 'Please, may I share this with you?'

Instead of just doing what you want to do.

Put on a smile when you enter a room;

Say, 'Please' and 'Thank you,' no matter to whom.

Ask for the things you want given to you,

And hold open doors for your friends to go through!"

So Jimmy said, "Thank you, I'll try it your way;

I'll do all I can do to try to obey."

And just as he said it, his hand gave a twitch

And seemed to get smaller—a small tiny bit.

"It's working!" said Jimmy, with hope in his eyes,

"I think it is shrinking back to its own size!

I promise I'll be more polite and to share,

To give of myself and to show that I care."

So Jimmy tried very hard, day after day,

To show his concern, to go out of his way,

To think more of others, and to say he agrees.

His hand seemed to shrink every time he said, "Please"!

He made many friends and found out it was fun

To finally feel good about things he had done.

He shared books with Jill and he gave toys to Jack,

And never said when he expected them back.

He held open doors for his teachers at school,

And tried hard to practice his new "Polite Rule":

JIMMY'S NEW POLITE RULE:

To try to treat others as I'd like to be,

To try to see things the way others might see,

To try to be helpful, and do what is right,

And to try at all times to be very polite!

JIMMY'S NEW POLITE RULE:

To try to treat others
as I'd like to be,

To try to see things the
way others might see,

To try to be helpful,
and do what is right,

And to try at all times
to be very polite!

27

As his hand got smaller, he made many friends;

Jack and Jill came to his house once again.

He found it was fun to share, rather than take;

He vowed never again to make that mistake.

For Jimmy knew better than to ever say, "Gimme";

Now none of his friends called him Gimme-Jimmy.

Finally, his hand matched the other he had.

"I'm very proud of what you've done," said his dad,

"Now that you've shown us this very big change,

We'll not call you Jimmy; you'll have to be James!"

Acknowledgements

As always, thank you to KJ and my wonderful illustrators at Kalpart.
They are awesome!
Thank you also to my publisher, SBPRA,
especially Robert and Lynn...
and also to Kait, Ellen, Linda and Denise

Special thanks to those
who have helped me share my books with children:
Julian, Verna, Yvonne, Lu, Rebecca and Barbara

Additional thanks to family and friends who have encouraged
and supported me along the way:
Kim, Kell, KC, John, Megan, Mary, Debbee, and Gez.

This book is also for my very special "prayer children" – Addie and Joey
And for all the Alexanders in my life:
Douglas Alexander, Sr., Jr., & III, Alexander Gilbert,
Paulo Alexandre, and Alexandre C.